PIG IRON

PIG IRON

PIG IRON

DUDREA PARKER
(MRS. SUMNER PARKER)

WILDSIDE PRESS

TO
MY MOTHER

Originally published in 1921.
Published by Wildside Press, LLC.
wildsidepress.com

CONTENTS

AN EPHEMERAL LOVE

Betty listlessly extended her hand to Walter; he bade her good-bye and strolled slowly homeward. That he was worried was evidenced by the nervous energy with which he smoked one cigarette after another until a box was consumed before he reached the door of his home, which stood on the hill leading to the railroad and bordering the fashionable district of Baltimore.

Was it Betty's interest in or love for another man that caused her apparent indifference, or was it his poverty that caused her to hold herself aloof from him? He knew full well that he had no luxuries to offer, yet the thought of her slipping from him forever made him desperate.

Walter was not visionary—he could not afford to be so; on the contrary, he was ultra-conservative, a quality not his by inheritance, but by compulsion. Since his father's death he had paid off some bills, supported his mother, saved a few thousand dollars, and managed to extend his business somewhat. Yet, as I say, luxuries were far from his reach—but tonight he craved them as never before. He condemned himself and attributed his poverty to his bovine stupidity. He was thirty and had a well-established lumber business, by means of which he believed another man could have attained wealth and position by this time.

These and similar thoughts passed through his mind—they come to all of us at times when our personal affairs loom so large upon our horizons— as he sat in his bedroom rocking on a straight-back chair. He was debating a big idea—a resolution to embark upon a business venture that had presented itself to him a short while before. It was not a speculation, but an original idea that involved risk, yet offered in return great wealth if it proved successful.

After an hour or more of deliberation he started to retire, entirely convinced that the proposition was feasible, and that tomorrow he would act upon his decision.

Nine o'clock found him in the office of the National Transportation Company.

"Son, is Mr. Bailey, your purchasing agent, here?" he asked of the clerk.

"Just this second come," answered the boy, showing Walter into the agent's office.

Mr. Bailey, a jolly-faced man, arose.

"Good morning; what can I do for you?" he inquired, pushing forward a chair.

"My name is Walter Gary. I'm in the lumber business and I've come to talk to you about dunnage. I understand that you are paying about twenty dollars a thousand feet for the rough plank lumber, which you use to separate and pack your cargoes of wheat for England."

"Yes," replied the agent.

"My business," continued Walter, "is wholesale lumber, and I represent large Southern mills, besides having a yard fairly well stocked on the water front. My proposition is to furnish you, without charge, lumber of good grade—ones, twos and commons, good lengths, which will make less work in separating cargoes, and being of good quality will be reasonably free from knots and shakes and much more satisfactory material to handle. However, we are not giving you something for nothing, although you will be free from expense in handling it. What we ask is that you deliver the lumber to our agents at dock in England when you have unloaded the wheat. You see, we both will profit by the transaction, as it will free you from your usual expense and at the same time will enable me to overcome the high rate of ocean freight."

The agent paced slowly up and down, with his hands thrust into his pockets, listening attentively to what Walter had to say. He was not an agent possessed of his own importance, as agents usually are, but made the situation easy by a kindly nod of his head at intervals—and with each nod Walter saw visions of his own home and Betty as its mistress.

"That sounds like a pretty clever scheme," he said, continuing to walk back and forth. "Can we always have dunnage when we want it? In other words can we depend upon you?"

"Most assuredly," answered Walter, in the tone of one accustomed to keeping his word. "We will furnish bond guaranteeing deliveries."

"Of course, it would have to be submitted to the president and directors before I could act, but if you care to put your proposition in writing and will return tomorrow at three, I shall try to get in touch with them immediately."

It was hard for Walter to conceal his elation. Was it possible that he had at last found a means by which he could ship lumber to Europe where it was greatly needed for building and rebuilding and where his agent could dispose of it at almost any figure—all without the exorbitant freight rates imposed since the war started and which had not yet been removed?

"I shall return at three tomorrow, Mr. Bailey, good-day."

"Good-day."

Walter stepped briskly into his office, did a little two-step, tossed his hat in the air, and said, "I have great hopes, Miss Franklin, great hopes."

The little typewriter smiled a smile of mingled interest and apprehension.

"I wish you good luck, Mr. Gary," she responded.

A full three-quarters of an hour elapsed while Walter waited the following day in the office of the National Transportation Company. Had Bailey forgotten his appointment? Had the directors accepted or rejected his offer? When would they take a consignment? He was thinking these and other thoughts, as he sat leaning in the chair, turning his hat around and around in his hands.

"Well, I've kept you waiting some time," said Mr. Bailey, hastily entering the office.

Walter tried to conceal his anxiety.

"You asked me to come at three, and I like to be on time, although I am in a bit of a rush."

"Yes, these are busy times for all of us. This question of feeding Europe is a perplexing one, aside from business transactions. Food stuffs must be rushed to the hungry ones at any cost. If you have been over seas you no doubt know how they need our help."

"No, I didn't get over," replied Walter somewhat dolefully. "I tried even before our country declared war. I wanted to go over with the Canadians: after I failed there and the U. S. took it up I tried again, but they turned me down, too. I have a dislocated shoulder and a broken knee cap—got them playing football at college; in fact, I was on my back two months with them. But I thought I was pretty well over it by this time—only feel it when the weather is bad."

"Those who wanted to serve and were rejected should have had a badge, stripe or something to show they were not slackers," sympathetically replied Mr. Bailey. "The country rejects the individual for things that are not his fault, and the world thinks as it pleases."

"Oh, well, it could have been worse. I did what I could at home putting Liberty Loans over, buying bonds, and making the soldiers comfortable in a general way, but none of it compensates for the real thing."

"Well, I think I've put the lumber deal through for you, although I had some difficulty doing it. Everybody is suspicious of free goods. I explained to the directors that your reason for giving the dunnage was to have it turned over to your London agent for disposal, after the cargoes were unloaded on the other side. They thought it a very fair proposition."

Bailey drew his chair nearer to Walter and smiled encouragingly.

"It will certainly serve both your purpose and mine," interposed Walter. "It will save you the expense of buying lumber with which to pack your wheat, and it will enable me to place quantities of it on the other side."

"A clever idea," repeated Bailey. "Can you have two hundred thousand feet delivered to me by Thursday?"

"I think so—by rushing like Sam Hill."

"All right, draw up your contract and get a move on you."

"I have already prepared it and have it here in my pocket. You see, I was hoping for the best."

The contract was signed, and he hurried to break the good news to Miss Franklin.

"If this plan is successful," said he, "you shall have a long vacation, and I—I have promised myself too much already—but if it fails! I tremble to think of the consequences."

"Mr. Gary," asked Miss Franklin, "are you sure there is such a wild demand for lumber on the other side as you say there is?"

"Yes, quite sure. My doubt lies in the question: Will Proctor be equal to the occasion! If this lumber is properly handled we should be able to make a million easily before the time expires."

"It's a big undertaking, isn't it," she said, astounded at the figure mentioned.

"Yes, but there is a big stake," responded Walter, and the little typist detected a note of sadness in his voice.

He hurried to disclose the good news to his mother, and as he pulled a chair to her side he patted her joyfully upon the cheeks, "Mother, perhaps we shall soon be rich," he said.

"Rich!" repeated Mrs. Gary, softly, yet in a tone of surprise. "I thought we were doing remarkably well for our bad beginning. Indeed, I was thinking only yesterday of what a comfortable feeling it was to have our debts paid and a little money laid away besides?"

"I—I used the money, Mother," confessed Walter, overcome with a feeling of remorse. "But I am quite sure to have it back soon, besides a great deal more. A big opportunity presented itself and I took advantage of it." Walter tried to appear more confident than he really was.

"What?" asked Mrs. Gary, in a voice that indicated alarm. "You have not used all the money, have you?"

"Yes, I used it on a big deal."

"Pray, what could such a deal be?" inquired Mrs. Gary, who had been more than apprehensive of her son's restlessness of late. As they talked together she quietly assorted remnants of wool, left from the many sweaters she had knit; and from her demeanor one could detect at a glance that she was a woman of composure and experience.

"Usually I prefer to tell you, Mother, before I take a leap, as you know, but this time I acted upon my own initiative."

"What have you done?"

Walter related to his mother, in detail, the story of his lumber transaction. He finished by saying, "You see the National Transportation Company have contracted to use my lumber for two years. Of course, I mean to send a good quality, and this will aid in reconstruction work on the other side and besides give us a big profit."

"I see," she responded, and gave her boy an admiring look.

"To carry out the program means sacrifice, and that's what is worrying me."

"The step is taken, so let us hope for the best," answered Mrs. Gary, cheerfully. "When do you deliver your first consignment!"

"Thursday, two hundred thousand feet."

Walter's mother arose, took her boy's face gently between her two hands, and looking steadfastly into his honest, dark eyes, said, "if you fail you have only done your best. Opportunities rarely present themselves. It is by the creation of them that men succeed. Half of success is grit."

"You are a dear brave 'sport.' The next time I shall not be afraid to consult with you on all my business problems."

"And I shall try not to retard progress."

"It gives me more courage to go ahead when I know you are in on the deal; things seem to turn out better."

"We all feel that way, dear. The troubles of life diminish when they are shared by others. Even the greatest becomes smaller when one knows that others are helping to bear it. It seems selfish, but misery loves company."

* * * *

"The cable, has it come yet, Miss Franklin?"

"Not yet."

Walter seated himself at his desk. There was a far away look in his face. "It should have been here four days ago. What do you think could be delaying Proctor?"

"Possibly it is the cable that's delayed, and not Mr. Proctor. Forget it, Mr. Gary, then it will be sure to come."

"How can I forget it when so much depends on that first consignment? I've hardly slept a wink since it was sent."

"You'll be a wreck if you keep worrying like this," rejoined the little stenographer.

"I'd be all right if I could only hear from Proctor."

Walter rose nervously from the chair at every turn of the door-knob. Would the thing never come? Surely, he must take Miss Franklin's advice and stop worrying about it. So he bade her close up, and strolled slowly homeward. He shrank from telling his mother again that he had had no word from London, for he knew only too well with what effort she was suppressing her anxiety.

He thought of diverting his course to Betty's office, but his better judgment caused him to continue; for he knew that even though Betty were ready to leave, some admirer would be waiting for her in his car, and she generally preferred riding to walking.

As he entered the door he heard his mother's voice softly singing a familiar tune; it encouraged him.

"Mother," he called, feigning indifference, "that darn thing hasn't come yet."

"Mr. Proctor appears to be having some difficulty in disposing of the goods, doesn't he?"

"I don't know what to think. Even if there was no market for the lumber, I should think he would wire."

"Never mind," suggested Mrs. Gary. "Don't cross bridges until you come to them. Go and see Betty this evening, she will cheer you up a bit."

"Oh, no, I'll wait and see if I make a success of this deal first; because if I lose, it will be good-bye to her anyway."

"Why good-bye! It will surely make no difference to her if you win or lose. I shouldn't think she was that sort of a girl."

"She's a fine girl, but she loves money and all it buys."

"No more than other girls; they all love money."

"But there is a difference. Take Sarah White for instance, the question of money isn't in her make up. She'd as soon marry Jack Evans and keep her position, if it would help, as not."

"Yes, I believe she would," affirmed Mrs. Gary, "but wouldn't Betty?"

"Never; she wouldn't marry the best man on earth unless he were rich."

"Perhaps she has never loved."

"Mere love of a man will never sway Betty."

"She has great aspirations—she loves luxuries, and the one who can supply them will be the one she will take."

"You do her an injustice. She never impressed me as having such exalted desires."

"But I know her so well. Yet with it all my one prayer is to be able to give her what she desires."

Mrs. Gary quickly dropped her work in her lap.

"Then you mean you love her, Walter?"

"Yes, I love her, her face is always before me—a vision that refuses to vanish!"

"I shall try to become better acquainted with her, dear, I had no idea she played such an important part in your life."

"She is a hard little trick to know."

"And feeling as you do, you say you have not spoken to her of your venture."

"No, because if I win I shall ask her to marry me. If I lose she shall never know that I love her."

Walter stooped, kissed his mother and walked slowly from the room, closing the door gently behind him.

* * * *

"What has become of you anyway!" asked Jack Evans as he appeared in Walter's office at lunch time. His entrance had not the slightest effect, however, upon the attention his friend and the stenographer were giving to a cable which apparently had just arrived. They did not raise their eyes from the sheet or give any sign of recognition until the last word had been read; then Walter waved the paper and said, "Three cheers!"

"What the dickens is the matter with you?"

"Read it," returned Walter, thrusting the paper into Jack's hand for him to read. "'Last of shipment disposed of. Good price. Order on hand for five hundred thousand feet.' It's the deal I was telling you of yesterday."

"Good work! have you another consignment going out soon?"

"Yes, and every dollar I own and a lot besides is tied up in a yard full of lumber waiting to be shipped."

"Lucky dog."

"I thought I was anything but lucky yesterday, after I had waited a week without a word from Proctor. Heavens, I thought I would go crazy. Last night I felt like swimming to England. I cabled him three times before he answered."

"Maybe you will play some golf with a fellow now."

"I am ready for anything. Want to play this afternoon?"

"Sure, at four. Meet me at the club. Oh, say, Betty was asking about you yesterday; she says she hasn't seen you for more than a week."

"What did she say and how did she look when she said it?" laughingly inquired Walter as they left the office.

"I told you what she said, you chump, and she looked as though she meant it. Why don't you quit working on that Bolshevism rot and join us occasionally at the club."

"I've been anxious about my business and besides Betty seems to be having a pretty good time without me."

"Nonsense, why don't you assert yourself? Women like to be bossed, you know." This was said in the tone of a person confident of his own powers along this line.

"Is that the way you manage Sarah? You surely have no kick coming where she is concerned."

"No, she's a brick, only she works too hard to suit me. Poor kid, she doesn't get in from Washington until five; then if she has an engagement at night, she is all in the next day."

"The satisfaction of knowing she is doing her bit compensates for that."

"Yes, and now that the war is over, I'm hoping we'll all be able to relax soon. I for one am sick of it all. The sight of a new man to train simply deadens me."

"Pshaw, Jack, what are you talking about? Aren't you proud the Hopkins students made such a good showing for themselves?"

"Yes, but I'm tired."

"How many of them got over anyway?"

"About three hundred and eighty in France, and approximately two hundred in the camps ready for service."

"Good, they have shown what they are made of, haven't they!"

"Yes, because many of them are only children."

"I envy them!" reflectively added Walter.

The two men parted. Jack was tall—at least six feet. He was slender and straight. He wore a Canadian uniform which showed off his figure to advantage. He also wore the D. S. C. ribbon, which was the envy of his men friends who had not seen service, and the glory and pride of all the girls upon whom he condescended to lavish attentions.

He had been assigned to Baltimore a year before to train college students for service. He found our clubs open to him, as were also the homes of our socially prominent families, because he was descended from a fine old Canadian family whose unimpeachable manners and traditions marked them unmistakably as of good English stock. These traits were prominent in Jack, and revealed themselves in his accent and cultured intonations.

Walter watched him out of sight, wondering why Jack had shown such a fondness for him, who was so entirely different. He compared Jack's graceful figure with his own, which was handicapped by a droop in one shoulder, and a limp. Often had Walter thought of his imperfections and promised himself to make up in knowledge what he lacked in form.

"Miss Franklin," said he, when he returned from lunch, "a little golf and tennis for me in the afternoons, but no other holiday this summer. I want you to run off and get rested up, because there will be lots of work for all of us soon."

"But you have already worked so hard, Mr. Gary, you ought to take a rest too."

12

"All of my wants are satisfied with this deal going through. It will not be long now before Gary & Co. will mean more than just a name to Baltimore."

* * * *

These days Walter's whistle sounded through the house like music to his mother's ears. He worked late into the night, but when morning came he was punctual and smiling.

"Love and business must be moving hand in hand with my boy," remarked Mrs. Gary at breakfast one morning.

"No, mother, I have seen very little of Betty in the last two months, but I have had a good many notes from her, and writing was something she never had time to do before—it indicates she's thinking of me, anyway."

"Possibly she is not working so hard now."

"Yes, she said she had only been to the club once in the last month, and you know how she loves to dance. She is sick of filing cards, poor kid. She is weary of her position. She is much too beautiful to be kept indoors. She would be able to live in the sunshine. It must be hard when one's friends are all able to take life so easily. Of course, the girls are all working now for the Government, but there's a difference between working for patriotism and for a living."

"Working for a living has its virtues; it's broadening, and she will learn things that are not taught at home."

"But she has that unconquerable yearning for life and its activities."

"That's all the better. She will learn to appreciate the advantages when they come to her, and she probably will never make the mistake of allowing her life to narrow down to one of domesticity, as so many young people do. If they could only learn that just as a landscape without a perspective is flat, so is a young life which has no outside interests to bring into relief the monotony of its daily tasks! Without a background of knowledge for comparison the unusual in life is flat and meaningless."

* * * *

Betty sat on the edge of her little white bed. It stood in a room simply furnished, and its whitish cast made a fitting background for her slight figure clothed in black with a plain white frill at the neck. Her eyes were slowly following the lines of a letter, which ran:

13

"DEAR BETTY:

"I send you roses to remind you that there is still much that is beautiful in the world—flowers and hills and sky, and nearer than these, home and family and friends. And there is much work to be done, work full worthy of your best, which just now you feel like giving to memory only; and there are so many lives to which your life may contribute something of what your mother gave to you.

"It is one of my abiding faiths that life must be forward-looking and onward-pressing, not with forgetfulness of those who have gone, but with strength and even happiness in the knowledge that we carry on their work and that they do not die; that through us, and through our children and friends, and all to whom we pass on something of what we received from them, they are borne on to everlasting life.

"For the moment we feel only the great loss—and today I feel as if something had gone from my life because so much has gone from yours—but sad as the moment is, it should also be one of the greatest moments of life; for from it should arise, purified from everything earthly, an ideal which may be as a torch to light the way. Thus among the most beautiful things still in the world are the spirits of those who have gone.

"With love,
"WALTER."

She folded the sheet that carried the consoling message—the only word that had helped her bear the loss of her mother and chum, whom she had seen buried but a few days before. She walked to the faded white roses which had accompanied it and which stood on a table close by. She touched them gently and then turned to the bed, and throwing herself on the pillow sobbed softly to herself.

Suddenly someone knocked gently upon the door.

How long had she been there? Rising she caught a glimpse of one very red cheek as she passed the mirror. She must have slept a long while.

"Why, Aunt Martha, what time can it be?" she inquired of a small kindly faced woman who stood outside the door.

"Eight-thirty, dear," her aunt replied, patting her on the arm. "Walter is waiting down stairs to know if you will see him for a moment."

"Yes, Marty," she said, using the pet name to compensate her aunt for climbing three flights of stairs. "I shall be right down." She closed the door, and sat down to think over the problem with which she was confronted. Her thoughts returned to the subject which occupied her mind before she fell asleep. She glanced at the letter which had fallen to the floor— such a message. Only one with a great heart could put such thoughts into words. There was no doubt in her mind that some day Walter would be a

14

"big" man. He had already accumulated a fortune, and his name was on the lips of all her friends. He loved her devotedly—that she was sure of, and he had been the favorite of her mother, who had cautioned her to think twice before she rejected him.

"And why shouldn't I marry him?" she asked herself over and over. "There is lots in life besides love. If he is willing to take me with a heart that is just friendly and accept other qualities instead of love, why shouldn't I make the deal for myself—just as he made one in lumber? He received large profits, and so would I. In return he gave good lumber, and I would supply good material as a wife. He signed a contract, and so will I."

She arose, bathed her face in cold water, carelessly twisted her hair low on her neck, and descended the stairs.

Walter stepped to meet her, she extended her hands, more cordially than she had ever done before, and he took them in his own. Never had he been so much in love with her. He gazed into the eyes that were of a surpassingly beautiful shade of brown. They looked larger than ever from grief and loss of sleep, and seemed to match the hair which clung to her forehead with a weblike softness. The nose was not large, but straight and well formed. The lips were a bit thinner and the mouth a bit larger than those an artist would choose for a model, but the even white teeth that had always been her salient attraction compensated for these deficiencies. These features went to make up a face that was not indicative of weakness, yet would not impress one as strong.

"I can't tell you how my heart goes out to you in your sorrow," he whispered softly.

"The letter, such a comforting letter," she answered, tears filling her eyes. "It helped more than anything."

"Then it has fulfilled its mission."

"How sweet of you to send the flowers," she added.

"It isn't a fraction of what I should I like to do for you. Betty, if you only knew how I love you! But there, I didn't come to worry you again. My new machine has just come, and I thought you might like a breath of air."

"How refreshing it would be," she answered. And she accepted with her eyes and turned to pick up a wrap. In fact, Betty was a flirt, and quite often her eyes said things that her lips did not confirm.

"What a monster in comparison with our little Ford," said she, as she sank into the softly cushioned seat beside Walter.

"Do you like it?"

"It's wonderful."

"Then I wish it was yours instead of mine."

"But then it would not be wonderful if you were not here beside me."

15

Walter gasped and almost ran into a passing machine. He looked down at the small figure beside him and asked. "Really—really, Betty, do you mean what you say?"

And in her heart Betty almost believed herself that she meant it.

* * * *

It was a season of reaction. War was over and with spring came the end of the winter festivities. Betty had derived much benefit from Walter's newly acquired fortune. There had been rides, dinners, flowers and everything dear to the heart of a girl. She found Walter's attentions the envy of other girls, and she reveled in the thought that he had eyes for no one but her—until she accepted his proposal of marriage and the wedding day was not far distant.

Then she revolted against the affection which she had obtained so easily, and which required such little effort to hold.

Jack often made the third party, and she found she liked it better when he was there. About Jack was a vagueness—an air of uncertainty and superiority that had always attracted her, even though he had paired off with Sarah.

As for Jack—deep in his heart there was the desire to prove to Betty that she could not number him among her many suitors. Yet recently he had been forced to admit that he liked and even sought her company.

It was a day brisk and cool for spring. Betty was in a perverse mood. She had whipped her dog without just provocation, and she had answered her aunt shortly several times that morning. The 'phone rang—it was Walter.

"Do you need me to help open packages?" "Why—no, Walter; there are only a few, and I'm so frightfully busy with the dressmakers that I can't stop just now."

"When you need me you'll call me, won't you, dear?" he asked, in a half pleading voice.

"Yes, I—I surely shall."

"This evening, may I come up?"

"I really ought to go to bed early; I'm so tired."

"Very well," he answered in a disappointed but conciliatory tone.

Betty slowly hung up the receiver, slipped into a scarlet sweater, and prepared for a walk in the country. The vivid color contrasted strongly with the pale cheeks, that had grown whiter and whiter of late. Her mind dwelt only on one subject. In two days the fatal knot would be tied—would she able to live up to the bargain? Could she give full pay for value received?

Walter, she knew, was the embodiment of gentleness and would make a good husband, but she craved for someone whom she must strive to win, and then plan to hold; neither had been necessary here. She had won him without competition, and now he was wholly at her command. "If only he were more elusive," she thought, "if only he went to places and did a few things without me."

"I miss the office dreadfully, Marty," said she between yawns.

"You always wanted to be out of it when you were there," answered her aunt in a tone of surprise.

"The work was drudgery, simply because filing cards required no brains. It was only repetition, but it was something to do."

"It will not be long that you will wish for something to do. Soon there will be work, work and more work."

"How can one work without an incentive?"

"An incentive! What more of an incentive could you and Walter wish than each other? You must conjure him to climb rung by rung to the top of the ladder, and that can be done only by setting a good example. A wife can lead her husband in paths that are good or bad. A man is more pliant than a woman, more susceptible to influence; therefore, she leads and he follows. One must be careful not to leave the other behind. Bear and forbear, and pull together."

"Walter is entirely too easily led," said Betty musingly.

"That's only because he loves you," said her aunt in absolute surprise, "and without the charms that were given you by God, you never could have won him. And remember, the seeds of love must be sown very deeply now, in order to hold him when your charms have failed. Beauty doesn't last forever, and age makes furrows in women's faces much quicker than in those of men. Men are out in the world where a variety of people and circumstances tends to keep them young; their minds are diverted, and they have no time for worry over petty annoyances, while women's minds become stagnant from the repetition of a daily routine. Their lives are confined within a narrow periphery, and there are only a few who enlarge the circle by wandering forth."

Betty hurriedly made preparations to be gone.

"Why will you not see Walter this afternoon when he wants so much to see you?"

"I just want to be alone," flung back Betty as she closed the door, but she had walked only a short distance when on turning the corner, she ran full into Jack. Always immaculately dressed, he wore the nonchalant air of a person who was confident that his appearance was an asset.

"And where is Walt this fine afternoon?" he asked, manifesting his pleasure at the chance meeting.

17

"He 'phoned a while ago, but I have to go to the dressmaker."

"Are you going to be there long?"

"Not so very."

"May I wait and will you take a walk with me? It's just the kind of a day for a walk."

"I think I should love to," she answered. And within she was conscious of both happiness and guilt.

She made haste and it was not long before she was back, sauntering slowly by Jack's side, and keeping in step without effort.

"Betty, do you know you walk like a boy, and don't we step nicely together?" Jack asked her, leaning down to peep into her eyes under the broad hat. "I've always heard that people who keep step uniformly are well matched," he continued.

"I believe I can keep step with most anyone," she answered, catching the significance of his words.

"But not so nicely as with me, I'm confident," he replied.

"Don't you hate to see the trees lose their leaves?" asked Betty to turn the subject, as she would divert a naughty child from something that exasperated it. "It is always such a sad season to me," she continued.

"Fall isn't always a sad season, but this one is especially so," said Jack wickedly, "because the trees are losing their leaves and so am I losing my little friend."

"Will I be lost, just because I'm married?"

"In a way."

"Oh no, you must come to see us even more often than you come now, and bring Sarah with you. By the way, where is Sarah? She has not been around for a week?"

"Indeed I don't know," was the indifferent reply, and this very attitude of indifference particularly pleased Betty. She resolved somewhere within her (if she could keep Walter from finding it out), to hold Jack's admiration at all costs.

They walked, chatted and laughed away the time until darkness completely overtook them. Walter did not hear of the little escapade; and if he had he was by nature too gentle, kind and unsuspecting to have thought long or hard of it.

After the wedding the young pair settled down in a lovely old colonial home, which spread itself against a hill in a rambling fashion. It was made conspicuous and inviting by a new coat of paint. Their choice had fallen upon this house, because of Betty's admiration of its finely detailed mantels, the broad stair, the quaint colonial windows, the box-wood garden, and the rustic spring house, with the little stream bordered by a row of weeping willows, whose boughs drooped so low that they seemed to be replenishing the brook with their tears.

Here Betty learned to know Walter. He taught her to love the out-of-doors. He patiently labored to teach her the correct strokes in golf and tennis, although he himself was handicapped in his participation in these games. In the evenings he tried to pick up the threads of his and her neglected education—he sought diligently to teach her to love the best in literature. And taking his life as a whole it centered about this little creature whom God had made too perfect in form and face.

Betty was fascinated and even entertained by the atmosphere of this new environment while it was new, but in the course of time she began to long for a change—adventure, and admiration for the world at large.

About two years after the marriage Jack paid one of his visits to the Garys. It was springtime, and the air was filled with the beauty of the season. Romance with her transforming wand had already touched Betty, and thoughts of Jack never failed to quicken her pulse.

It was his fourth or fifth visit since Christmas; and each time Walter and Betty had welcomed him wholeheartedly.

Jack had risen early this morning prepared to take a long walk, and had been served a cup of hot coffee before starting. He was, as usual, perfectly dressed. One could not call him vain; yet he had an inherent desire to appear handsomer, more learned, and more of an athlete, in the company of Betty than he really was.

Going down the drive he heard a happy peal of laughter. It was childish, yet more mellow and appealing in its ring. Looking around Jack perceived the slight figure of Betty perched high in a tree. She was climbing higher with the agility of a squirrel, stepping from limb to limb and frolicking among the branches like a young animal, that had not yet been burdened with the care of gathering food or preparing for winter shelter. On limbs lower down were two small boys of about eight and ten, children of the overseer. They had already become Betty's playmates, and were making a desperate effort not to be outdone by her. Jack gave a long low whistle. Betty clung closer to the trunk of the tree and then peeped out, disclosing to view one eye and a part of her dishevelled hair. In answer to the whistle she encircled her mouth with her hand and called, "It's too early for anyone to be up yet."

"May I climb up there?" called back Jack softly.

"No, I'm all disarranged."

"Please let me," he pleaded.

"I'm coming down this minute," answered Betty, lowering herself to the ground.

"Will you walk a little with me?" asked Jack, bound not to lose her for the two long hours before the morning meal.

"I'm only in bloomers," answered Betty still protecting herself from view.

"They are all the better for walking—come with me, the air is wonderful."

"Come along then."

In less than a minute Jack was by her side. "How adorable," he remarked, as he caught his breath and surveyed the small figure before him attired in a middy blouse, bloomers and sneakers.

"Is it bad for me to walk with you so early without Walter," she asked slyly, pretending not to know.

"Why what's bad about it? It isn't premeditated, and I'm not going to abduct you."

"Abduct me," repeated Betty, "I never thought of such a thing."

"But I have," Jack replied, complacently. "I'd steal you this very second, if I dared."

"If you talk like that, Jack, I shall not stay with you."

Jack's persistence in making intimate and affectionate remarks served apparently to discompose Betty at times, although more than once she was conscious of having feigned annoyance. But now she turned quickly and started toward the house. Jack leaped forward and caught her by the wrist.

"Don't be prudish," he pleaded.

"But you say such disrespectful things to me," pouted Betty.

"I didn't mean to; please forgive me."

Betty yielded and they started off again over the hills at a brisk pace.

"Let's run a race," suggested Betty.

"All right, we'll start at the foot of the hill, and race to the second big tree."

"May I have a handicap?" asked Betty.

"Yes, to the little rock just there," said Jack, pointing to a stone a few feet away.

"Oh, that isn't enough," grumbled Betty.

"It's all you can have," answered Jack in his usual decided manner. "Don't start until I say three. One—two—three."

They were off. Betty sprang up the hill like a deer. Jack gradually overtook her, but when she heard him gaining on her, she summoned all of her remaining strength and fairly leapt over the ground. Jack pulled ahead and won by only a few paces—and he had done his best. She backed to the tree for support while Jack threw himself to the ground.

"Ah, you're all out of breath."

"Not a bit of it," answered Jack, jumping to his feet. "Why are—are you using the tree for a prop?"

"But I didn't fall down and I'm not out of breath."

Jack moved to her side, drew her arm through his, and said, "Come on, little boy, you did very well, and I love you against that tree."

"I believe I shall stay by the tree," she added wickedly, glancing into Jack's face to see if he caught the significance of her words.

Quick as a flash he answered, "The tree isn't necessary. It is the same anywhere."

A flash of deep scarlet rose to Betty's cheeks, as she realized that, for the first time in her acquaintance with Jack, she had deliberately invited his advances. And though a feeling of joy surged through her being at the thought of it, she was conscious of a deep sense of shame on realizing that she, who had always esteemed herself above such practices, had not only allowed another than her husband to make open advances to her, but had even encouraged him to do so.

"Please will you tell me the time?" she asked, with eyes averted.

"Just ten minutes after eight."

"We must be hurrying along," she said, quickening her step, "breakfast will be served, and besides we're very bad."

"Bad," repeated Jack, "why bad?"

"Because it is bad for us to be speaking this way to each other—I'm deceiving Walter—I didn't mean to say what I said."

"But I meant what I said," replied Jack, in his habitual positive tone, "and what's more I can't help it. Love is the only thing in life that can't be regulated. It comes and goes unbidden. To work or to be idle, to be kind-hearted or cruel, to accustom ourselves to outdoor or indoor lives is ours to decree, but to love or not to love is beyond the power of any human being, and right at this moment I am loving you more than I ever loved any one in all my life.

"What causes this great love," he continued philosophically, "I am at a loss to know. Candidly I should much prefer to love Sarah, because I believe she loves me, and besides she is not encumbered with a husband."

"Walter is not an inc—."

"Tell me honestly, Betty dear," interrupted Jack, "do you want me to love you, or must I go away?"

"I think you must go away." But she wished he would not take her at her word.

"When?"

"I—I don't know," she stammered, restraining her tears.

"But you care, don't you? Admit it, do admit it. Admit it so that I can go back to my work and accomplish something." He had not yet felt the sting of a troubled conscience, nor did he realize that the inconstancy of his friend was drawing a cloud around her life that might never be cleared away.

Betty stepped closer to the man, who had so dominated her will. She looked straight into his compelling eyes, and the words which she wanted to say failed her. She felt that she could not see him go from her, yet she knew that there was no comparison between him and her husband; that her husband possessed all the qualities of a strong and good man that the other man lacked.

Walter sat reading the morning paper. Jack paced slowly up and down on the veranda. The family gathered for breakfast. Betty appeared in a fresh yellow muslin, relieved by a snow white collar and sash. As she descended the stairs Walter laid aside the paper.

"Aren't you going to church, dear?" he asked. "I thought you would be ready by this time."

"Can we leave Jack?" her heart jumping at the mere mention of his name.

"Make him go along," responded Walter.

"He doesn't like church; and especially on a day like this, I am sure he would rather be out of doors."

"Oh, well there is lots for him to do—ride, play golf, anything he likes. We'll be gone but a short time."

"Can't we worship in the open today? It's so wonderful out-of-doors."

"It is wonderful," replied Walter, drawing out Betty's chair for her, "and it does seem hard to shut one's self up on a day like this. But there is no getting around it—there are certain duties we owe to the Creator of these wonderful days, and there is only one day in the week on which we can openly pay them. If I evade them I am conscious all the week of having neglected my duty. It's all right, dear, to say let's worship in the open, but we just don't do it. Once off, that's the end of it."

"Oh, come, Walt, don't make me feel like a heathen," interposed Jack. "I don't mind going to church, but it's the everlasting long sermons we are subjected to, that I dislike."

"I admit it isn't the sermon that attracts me; I go simply to offer my thanks, and—and to worship in a way, although I must confess that it is the whole service that does me good—the sermon, the hymns and the prayers. It's like taking a shower on a hot day."

"It is indeed," remarked Aunt Marty. "I can tell you children from experience, that material things do not satisfy when one is nearing the end of life. It's the good we've done and the trust we've had on the journey, and it is that worship that Walter speaks of that stimulates and inspires us to do the good and have the trust."

"How about driving in to hear Dr. Burk this morning? He isn't afraid of the truth, and will tell us something worth listening to, I am sure. Jack, you'll like him; come along, and we'll have golf right after dinner."

"I'll play you some golf, but I am going to renig on the church proposition. I've strayed too far from the fold to be gathered into it now. May I borrow Delphie and go for a ride?"

"Sure, I'll have Frank saddle her for you," answered Walter.

The meal was finished; Aunt Marty left hastily to make ready for church. Betty lingered in the conservatory rearranging a few stray ferns.

"Dear, are you going?"

"Have I time to dress? It's so late already."

"Well, leave the plants alone and hurry."

"Walter dear, if you don't mind I think I shall stay at home. There are lots of little things I want to do and when they are finished perhaps I'll ride a little with Jack."

"No, don't let me keep you home," interposed Jack, trying to appear disconcerted at Betty's indecision.

"As you like, dear," answered Walter, "only be careful with Ringgold, she is as wild as a hare—she hasn't had exercise lately."

"You are sure you won't mind?" asked Betty pleadingly, as she steadily looked into Walter's eyes, for she knew his power of observance and his ability intuitively to arrive at conclusions which were often startlingly correct.

"I'm satisfied if you are," he answered.

Betty was conscious of a feeling of guilt as she watched the two men go down the room side by side—Walter, a bit stooped, bald and slightly limping, Jack, tall, straight, thin, with a mass of dark hair. Her cheeks burned as she thought of her subterfuge, and felt herself drifting into deception.

"I'll take good care of the little lady, Walt," Jack was saying, as the car whisked away.

Jack lingered about on the veranda; Betty disappeared and did not return until she heard the low, long, familiar whistle come from the foot of the stairs. At that moment she appeared on the landing.

"Do come and talk to me, little boy?" begged Jack in a soft, loving tone.

"I'm sorry I didn't go to church," answered Betty regretfully, as she slowly descended to the lower step. This brought her head to a level with Jack's shoulder.

"Did you stay for my sake? Don't be stingy—say yes," he coaxed.

"No—no indeed, there was lots to be done here."

23

She stepped back up the stairs, half disgusted at both her own and Jack's actions. She tried not to be one of those helpless girls who unconsciously betray themselves, and whose behavior is controlled solely by their impulses. She could not comprehend in what manner she had become apathetic toward Walter—Walter who was so tender, thoughtful, and true to her. She would have expressed the utmost surprise and disapprobation if she had heard that another had been detected in this immodest affair—if indeed, she had believed it possible.

"I stayed because I did not like to leave my guest alone, and because I really had things to do."

"But I am vain enough to think that had I not been here the 'things to do' would have remained as they were."

As Jack made this assertion he drew Betty gently back to him and pressed his lips to the top of her head. She stood as if held by a vice.

"Please—please, Jack, won't you help me to be good? I owe so much to Walter."

"Money is money, my little boy, but there is no such thing as a love debt. We know not where love goes or whence it comes. We only know that it has come to you—and to me. It has caught us as fish are caught in a net, and I can think of no escape."

"But we must do something. Can't we pray for guidance?"

"No—I can only pray that in some way I shall soon be able to make you mine."

Again he kissed the top of her head, and as she turned to resist him, he folded her slowly but closely into his arms. She yielded—their lips met, every nerve and fibre tense in the two young bodies.

"You were mine in heaven, darling, long before you came to earth. I lost you—and all these years I've been searching for you; now I've found you, never, never to let you go—mine—you must be mine."

"Oh, Jack, how can I ever look at Walter again?" sobbed Betty, tearing herself away. "I can never make my peace with God and him," she said brokenly. "I shall always be afraid in the day lest my actions betray my guilt, and at night I shall be afraid to sleep for fear some self-accusing word may escape my lips."

"It would be cruel for me to subject you to such misery," said Jack, leading her to a comfortable couch, which stood before a large open fire. "Come with me—come until we can arrange to be each other's?"

"Leave—leave Walter?" she asked, as if half dazed. The words seemed crude—unreal, if she had suddenly awakened from a dream whose content was even now vague and fast fading into the subconscious.

"Come, darling, we'll solve it later," said Jack, holding her closer in his arms. "My little boy is so frightened now."

His words and movements indicated possession. She was now the ruling passion of his life—.

* * * *

It was with great trepidation that Betty awaited the return of Walter; she still had time to rectify her wrongdoing and send Jack away forever. This action was in her power and she was fully conscious of its importance. And her chief thought was of the sorrow she was about to bring upon the man who had been father, husband and brother all in one—who had lived but to please her; surely she was listening to the mad promptings of a wild impulse. Then she strove to persuade herself that Walter was phlegmatic and plain, a person whose goodness consisted rather in the avoidance than the overcoming of temptation.

"Direct me, God, to the right choice," said she aloud.

Jack held her at arm's length and austerely scanned her features.

"Dearest, you know you love me—the joy of this hour is proof enough: these thrills are the thrills of love; the first that have ever come to you or to me. Come, dear, come with me. Do not leave my soul in anguish—my heart famished. Darling, come and I shall protect you always. Answer, my own—answer yes," whispered Jack, as his lips repeatedly pressed warm kisses to hers—and the answer came slowly and softly—"Yes, I'll come."

"When? Now?"

"No, I must make it easy for Walter first. I must arrange things and it will take a long while."

"I'll be waiting for you, sweetheart, and even if my body be exiled from you forever my heart will still be yours."

* * * *

An epidemic of "flu" had spread over the country—multitudes were sick and dying. Many of the doctors had not returned from the war and the few left were inadequate in numbers to cope with the dreaded malady.

Dr. Baker looked up at his wife from the couch where he had fallen from exhaustion.

"Dear," said she, "there is another desperate case in the Valley. Do you think you can possibly go out tonight? They are waiting at the 'phone for your answer."

"Tonight! Not possible, Jane, I'm so tired I can scarcely walk another step. Tell them to try Johnson; they will just about catch him. Who is ill?"

25

he asked, as his wife was leaving the room.

"Mr. Gary—Walter Gary."

"Walter Gary?" repeated Dr. Baker, sitting upright.

"Yes."

"Ask how long he has been ill."

Mrs. Baker returned almost immediately. "It's Mrs. Gary at the 'phone; she is begging you to come. She says her husband has just been taken, but he seems desperately ill."

The doctor pulled himself to his feet.

"He's just about the age and the build of the ones who go quickest."

"Mrs. Gary said she would send for you at once if you would come," continued his wife.

"Never mind, tell her I'll be there as soon as I can make it."

It was the latter part of the following week. Dr. Baker entered his home at midnight as noiselessly as possible, but his wife was waiting for him and accosted him from the top of the stairs.

"Is he better, Dick?"

"No, Jane, I'm afraid we're going to lose him after all. I came home only to snatch a wink of sleep and shall be returning directly."

"And you really think he is going to die?" asked Mrs. Baker, as she took her husband's bag from him.

"It looks that way," answered the Doctor, resignedly. He had become more or less callous to sickness and death, but this case, as he described it, was a very appealing one. He regarded young Gary as the combination of all that went to make a fine citizen, husband, and son, and to be cut down when he hadn't well begun to live was more than he could understand.

"Perhaps he'll pull through yet," said Mrs. Baker, but the doctor only shook his head as he wearily stretched himself out on his bed for a short rest.

When he entered the sick room the next morning the blinds were drawn low to keep out the glare of the bright morning sun. Two figures in white moved noiselessly about the room. He seated himself beside the bed and gravely regarded his patient. There were two tanks of oxygen, basins, towels, and a few dishes here and there, and fumes of a disinfectant were plainly detectable as one crossed the threshold. All went to make up an atmosphere wherein a very ill or dying patient lay.

Betty stood opposite the doctor, her eyes sunken and her face white and drawn; with one hand she held pitifully to Walter, while the other clutched convulsively at her throat.

"Dr. Baker, do something more—for God's sake do something for him," she pleaded, "Walter—Walter," she called softly, but earnestly. Then she threw back her head in despair and prayed ardently to God to save her husband.

"Save him, dear God. Do as you will with me, but save him." She ended in a husky voice.

The realization of her profound love for her husband thrust itself upon her very forcibly in these hours when his life hung by a thread.

"All has been done that human hands can do, dear girl," spoke the doctor quietly beside her.

Walter slowly opened his eyes and said, "Baby—I'll—be—waiting—for—you." The breath came in short, quick gasps and the eyes closed for the last time. Betty called and called, but no answer came—the voice was hushed forever.

An hour later they carried her limp form from the room. On regaining consciousness she sat up in bed and called again, "Walter—I want to go back with Walter."

"But you musn't, Mrs. Gary," soothingly spoke the nurse at her side. "You can't do him any good, and you must not jeopardize your own life more than you already have."

"I—I—want to go," groaned Betty. "They will take him from me soon, forever. Oh, my darling, my darling."

"Rest awhile, you've been through so much," pleaded the nurse. "Think, dear, don't you want to help rid the community of this dreadful disease? It's spreading so wildly that we must all do our part to eliminate it."

"No—no," sobbed Betty, "I only want to go with him—with him—with him—."

Two months passed. Betty, pale, thin and worn by sickness and grief, walked arm in arm with Aunt Martha through the paths of the old fashioned garden. One glimpse of the grief-stricken girl would leave in the mind a picture one could never forget. The large eyes looked out from depths much deeper than ever before; the ashy pale cheeks made a startling contrast to the dark eyes. The figure was thin almost to emaciation and the dress was simple and black. The mischievous expression was replaced by one of listlessness and altogether she looked like one who had but a slender hold on life.

"Marty, do you think Dr. Baker would allow me to ride Walter's horse alone?"

"Not today, you're not strong enough yet. I wrote Jack that you might be well enough to see him today. He is coming out on the early train."

"I wish I didn't have to."

"He'll cheer you up, dear. I've been looking forward to his visit. Walter liked him and you've put him off so often. Now let him come."

"I would rather not see anyone," responded Betty, her eyes filling with tears.

"But Jack has been so thoughtful—see him for me. You'll feel better for having had a little company."

Slow steps sounded on the gravel path. Betty darted a look like a frightened deer in the direction from which they came. Jack approached them between an aisle of poplars.

"Have I caught you unawares?" he asked jocularly, and his face showed plainly that he was startled at the changed appearance of Betty.

"Oh no," answered Aunt Marty, "my girl has just been asking for a horse-back ride."

"I wanted to ride Walter's horse alone for a little while," interposed Betty sadly.

"You are not strong enough to do that," said Jack.

"But I'd like to."

"Take care of her, Jack," said Aunt Marty, indicating a seat at the far end of the garden. "I must go and see about my chickens—two of my prettiest white ones were killed by a train."

"Mrs. Ames," Jack called laughingly after her, "can't you train chickens better than to have them stand on a railroad track?"

The figure of the patient little old lady disappeared among box woods.

"She didn't hear me," he added, turning to Betty.

"She has three hundred and they all seem to know her," answered Betty, relieved for the moment to find something impersonal to talk of. "Would you like to see the new puppies? There are five of them, Frank says. I haven't seen them myself yet."

"No, dear girl. I want to see you and you only. Why have you avoided me, when you know my heart has been aching so badly? and that I love you so deeply?"

Betty rose slowly from the bench, waved Jack away with her hand, and was about to leave him. "Please, will you never, never breathe a word—of—love to me again," she asked.

"What?" asked Jack. "Were you only playing with me, Betty?"

"No—before God, I knew not what I did or said."

"Come, come, my little girl, you are weak and faint—I'm a brute to worry you. Let's be friends now and sweethearts later."

Betty shuddered at the mention of the word.

"No," she answered, shaking with emotion—"never have I been your sweetheart, and my grief is that I never realized how truly I did love Walter. He was ever present, dependable, and true. I felt that I could put out my hand in the dark and he was always there to guide and help me, yet I shunned that hand, and deliberately planned to ruin him—to ruin him—just as if I had been his worst enemy. The things one is sure of are the things one casts aside, and I, like a venturesome child, reached for those that were forbidden."

As she talked her breath came more evenly; the stricture around her heart relaxed, she leant back in the garden seat, as she felt her throat tighten and tears rising to her eyes. She could not keep them back; she was not strong enough. They fell and fell, and from time to time she brushed them away with her handkerchief.

"Then you've stopped—loving me—my little boy has stopped loving me," Jack repeated mechanically.

"It was only an ephemeral love—can you forget it and me?" she asked, gently touching his arm. Like the balmy air of spring was the gentleness of her presence beside him, and, unrelenting as she was, it was enough that she was there.

"And you'll never be mine?" Jack added, turning again to look into the eyes that held the world for him.

"No—I am married. My husband is dead, but I am married and always shall be. I was not true to him while I had him for my own, but the veil is lifted from my eyes and until we see each other again I am his. For God knows that I loved him."

At these words a peaceful expression settled upon the pale face, and Jack saw and realized that whatever of shallowness her nature had contained had been consumed in the flame of her tragedy. The real Betty was before him, showing the honesty, the nobility, of her true spirit—depth had taken the place of shallowness. She had lost and suffered and this made her still dearer to him, and sacred. He felt the urgings of his better nature bidding him to forget self in the presence of this sorrowing woman. And he saw that his love could not be—that his relationship to her henceforth would have to be on a more unselfish plane.

They slowly retraced their steps through the aisle of poplars.

"May I still be to you what Walter should have liked me to be?" asked Jack tenderly, and the answer came distinctly, "Yes, his friend and mine."

29

"THE WHITE PETAL"

There never lived another man so utterly unreliable as Albert Wilbur. If he promised to be at a certain place at a certain time one could count definitely on his absence. But I never thought he would overlook an appointment as important as that which he had made to meet me at his country house on the night of August 3, 1919.

The two Wilbur boys—John and his adopted brother, Albert—were from childhood my most intimate friends, and I often found it necessary to help Albert out of serious difficulties.

As a boy he was exceptionally handsome and promising, but the vices to which he succumbed in later years not only robbed him of his good qualities, but also brought upon his friends lasting sorrow; for when I last saw him his indulgence in depravities had nearly approached a continuous performance.

John, my real chum, was the embodiment of manhood—the only thing I had against him was that he married my childhood sweetheart. Her name was Ellen. My love for her was real, it was deep, and it was earnest. Let me say it was no passing fancy, for there had never been anything to approach it until now. However, I was not blind to John's qualities, and was compelled to admit to myself on more than one occasion that in selecting a husband Ellen had only shown her usual good judgment.

Since this catastrophe in my life I had retired into myself, determined to live a life of single blessedness. I resolved to consign to oblivion this period of my existence—existence I say, because this word most nearly describes my life at this time. I first tried hard work as a means to aid me in my purpose. This helped, but did not entirely fulfill the essentials. I discovered that what I needed was a change, a new environment: so I pulled up stakes, hard as it was to leave my three friends—for their little girl was just eleven, and had become my closest companion—and spent the next seven years roaming about the world, finding my pleasures in nature, books, new scenes and old cathedrals.

I had heard regularly from the Wilburs since my departure, but my sudden return was due to the last letter—it was written by a friend of the family. She informed me of a fatal automobile accident in which both John and Ellen had lost their lives. In sequence to this was a telegram from Albert. On my arrival in New York more letters from him awaited me. It was at least a week, however, before I started South for my ultimate destination. I gathered all my belongings—for something told me I would not soon return—and prepared for a rapid departure.

The night was cold for mid-summer, and I remember distinctly how I drew my raincoat about me as I walked from the gate across the lawn to where a dim light glowed through the trees. I had dismissed the carriage which had brought me from the lonely station, as our business was of a somewhat secret nature, and so much had been exchanged between us in regard to it that I counted on finding my friend waiting. As I brushed through the mist-laden shrubbery, I thought how welcome would be the grasp of his hand after so many years of separation, and how quickly the warmth of his presence would dispel the strange uncanny loneliness which had crept upon me during my long ride through the woods, with never a sound except the gentle patter of water dropping from the trees and the slop—slop of the horse's hoofs in the mud of the road.

So I was more than annoyed, in fact, I was hurt and disgusted when the decrepit old fellow who had always been a part of the Wilbur household informed me that "Mister Albert" had wired that he would not be there until the morning. "Very sorry," the wire ran, "impossible to keep appointment with Constable. Make him comfortable for night. Will be on in morning. 'For Constable: Do forgive me, old fellow, and make yourself at home. You have the place to yourself. Guarantee no ghosts.'"

"Small comfort," I murmured to myself, not being able to repress a sneer—the note was so characteristic of its author.

"Very good, sir," said the spectre beside me, whose presence I had almost forgotten. "I have moved your bed into the library here, where there is an open fire. You'll find whiskey and soda right on the table, and I'll put your bag close by the bed. Anything else you'd like, sir?"

"No thanks, Watkins," I said, recovering the old fellow's name from some recess in my memory. "I shall do very well, no doubt. But I'm disappointed."

"Yes, sir, yes, sir," and with these words Watkins disappeared.

"I'll be damned," I muttered. "This is getting positively spooky."

I looked down—a big mastiff pup, overgrown and generally loppy in appearance, evidently thinking himself addressed, arose slowly from the hearth rug and came towards me, wagging the entire rear end of his body in a gesture which seemed exaggerated at the time, though I have no doubt now that even that did not convey the real extent of his pleasure in having company.

"Well, old man," I said, stroking his head, "it doesn't seem so bad here, after all. Here's looking at you," and I sipped the glass of warming spirits that Watkins had poured for me. After the last drop had been swallowed I

31

seemed to remember that Watkins had cast some apprehensive glances at this very glass before he left the room.

"Nonsense," said I to myself, "it's all imagination," and I continued, "with a good fire, a good drink, and a good book, what more does man want, unless it be a dog? That's where you come in, old chap," and I reached down and patted him. "Let's see what there is to read," I continued, still addressing the dog for the sake of company.

Albert had one peculiar trait; he always took an austere pride in being a man of few books, and those such as no one else could understand. So I found little help in the scattered but much-thumbed volumes lying in odd corners about the room. Psychology, metaphysics, and a few seventeenth century works on alchemy made up the entire collection.

I was beginning to feel sleepy, so I chose the book with the largest print, and sat down before the blazing fire to while away the hours until slumber overtook me.

The inevitable happened: I fell asleep in about five minutes.

I awoke with a feeling of suffocation. The clock on the mantle was chiming twelve, and I counted the strokes, which seemed to be a continuation of something I had been dreaming. Ten, eleven, twelve, I said aloud dreamily, like a child repeating a lesson. And then a strange thing happened. The clock struck, most distinctly, thirteen, and with a whirring sound stopped dead, the second hand resting exactly in line with the hands of the dial, which pointed to midnight.

"Are we asleep or awake, old man?" I again addressed the dog, trying to pass the thing off as a joke, and stretched out my hand to pat his head. A low growl startled me. The pup was standing erect, every muscle tense, his ears cocked forward, and the hair on the back of his neck bristling. The growl continued for a moment; then a change gradually came over him. The growls became a kind of pitiful whine, his head fell with drooping ears, his tail dropped between his legs, and trembling in every limb he crept to my feet and reached his nose up between my knees, while in his poor dumb eyes, pleading with me as only a dog's eyes can plead, were registered the terror that I suddenly realized I was sharing with him. Strange unspoken communion of man and beast.

At that moment the seeming impenetrable silence of the night was rent, like a flash of lightning across a pitch-black sky, by a woman's shriek. No, not a shriek, but a wail, a piercing appeal that nothing could describe. It had all the lure of the Lorelei and the despair of the Siren spurned, and yet all the sweet timbre of a child's instinctive call to a sleeping mother. Then silence, the absolute and unbounded silence of the grave.

Quivering in every nerve, scarcely able to stand as it seemed at the time, yet impelled by some unknown force, I found myself running through strange passages, wrestling with the darkness, on and on, guided I know not how straight to her whose appeal had come to me—to me of all the people in the world—this night of August 3, sharp on the stroke of—thirteen! Then I was battling with some unknown, unseen opponent, lunging forward wildly, whirling, heaving; and finally with a terrific wrench, which exhausted the last ounce of strength in my body, I threw off my foe, threw him off with such force that he seemed to be shattered in the darkness beyond, and the air that I drew into my lungs in gasping gulps was pure of the evil of his breath.

Silence again, as I stood leaning against the balustrade trying to regain my senses. What had happened; was it all a bad dream? Then slowly I became conscious of a weight against my knees, of two clinging arms about my waist, of a sweet perfume like that of an old-fashioned garden in the dewy twilight; and a soft childlike voice was saying:

"O, please, what is it; what has happened, oh, please—"

The soft voice trailed off into a sob, and the arms tightened about me. I reached down and picked her up, a clinging trembling little form, its gentle curves rounding into womanhood. How she clung to me, poor frightened little soul, her arms tight about me and her cold little face buried against my neck. Then, as I made my way back to the library, she rested quietly, like a white petal blown from the garden and storm-tossed, but at last at peace. I could feel her warm tears and the fresh moist little spot that was her mouth. She seemed to be murmuring something; or did her lips move gently in a kiss?

I slowly regained my senses, which seemed to be numbed and deadened but a short time before. My body felt as though pins and needles were sticking me. My breath came more evenly. I held her lithe, supple little form at arm's length and scanned the features carefully. I could not believe my eyes—was it little Ellen? Could it really be? Yes, the features were almost the exact reproduction of her mother's. The straight nose, the well formed lips and the appealing grey eyes, fringed with straight, long lashes —all of these I took in at a glance. I was still too weak to drag ourselves far from the assailant, but her weak little voice whispered, "Run, Don Compie! Run!" The frightened look in her eyes and the commanding appeal of the words served to restore my senses.

Was it a blow from the opponent that had deadened me or was it the whiskey and soda that had done the trick? It was the dose, because I remembered with what difficulty I aroused myself from the drowsy sleep that was about to overtake me. I held Ellen closer to me and made off as fast as my clumsy feet would move. We were well into the cold woods, through which I had ridden but a few hours before, when she said, "I can walk now, please put me down." I slid her gently to her feet, she slipped her hand into mine, and we fled as though savages were pursuing us. As we ran she murmured between breaths, "Watkins told me he had seen Uncle Albert put something in the whiskey that was on the table. I was trying to reach you when he seized me. He has kept me a prisoner since I refused to marry him. Today is my birthday and the day you were to become my guardian."

"Yes," I answered, "but he wrote me you had disappeared—had eloped, been kidnapped or something."

"It wasn't true—I'll tell you all about it when we are safe—safe and far from this dreadful place."

We traveled hours before we were on the highway. The damp but invigorating air had restored me and the child seemed possessed of unusual endurance. I espied in the distance a small farm house. A light was shining through a window on the side. The thought came to me that, although it was still dark, perhaps they were preparing breakfast. "Ellen," I said, "before we go further we must have something to eat."

"Bread and milk will do," she answered.

"Let us inquire here," I rejoined.

"But suppose Uncle Albert should follow us?"

"Now that we are out of that hornet's nest I rather wish he would. I must meet him face to face and have this out!"

"No, Don Compie, please! please! he might get me again," she pleaded. "I would much rather die." She clung to my arm tightly as we made our way to the farm house. I knocked, the door was opened by a kindly faced, stooped-shouldered old man in his shirt sleeves. I told him my daughter and I had met with an accident about five miles back in the country, and were walking to the nearest garage—would he accommodate us with a little breakfast. He looked at me long and searchingly—I say long, perhaps it was only a second; then as if satisfied with the examination, he said yes, if we didn't mind cooking the bacon, he could give us some bread, milk and apple-butter. But his wife had died two months ago, and his boys had already gone to the field to plough and were waiting for him; so there was no one to wait on us. "But just make yourselves at home," he added, as he shuffled about in thick soled boots, pouring what was left from a can of milk into an earthen pitcher, and placing a large loaf of bread before us. "Them automobiles," and he shook his head disgustedly, "when they make up their minds to stop, thir's just no way setten thim up again, is thir? No, sir, gimme a pair of mules any day, they're stidier."

"My engine went wrong this time, and I simply can't get the thing started. I'll have to be towed in, I'm afraid."

"Just shut the door when you get done, and if you want water you can fetch it from the pump yonder."

34

I took pains to thank him and pay him for his hospitality, and promised to close up carefully.

Ellen, minus a hat, sat with her elbows on the table and her chin in her hands, while the old man moved about putting things a bit in order, as he called it, before he left. "Since the missus died, I have to look after everything inside and outside." This he said as he brushed the crumbs from the preceding breakfast on to the floor, and then swept crumbs, dirt and all out of the door.

After he disappeared down the hill, behind the pump, Ellen raised her eyes appealingly to mine. "What am I to do, Don Compie?" This was the name she had given me when she was a baby and could not say John Constable. Her mother, too, had called me by it in later years, to distinguish me from her husband.

As I have said, it was seven years since I left for Europe in one last effort to forget her, whom fortune decreed I could not possess. When I left little Ellen was just a child, almost a baby. But now she was blooming into womanhood.

"Ellen, dear," I asked sympathetically, "do you feel strong enough to tell me of the death of mother and daddy? Were you in the motor with them at the time of the accident, or just how did it happen?"

"No," she answered slowly, and unrestrained tears flowed freely down the pale cheeks, "they were alone with Peter the chauffeur, returning from Upper Falls. Peter turned into the railing of the bridge to avoid another machine, which was coming very fast—the railing gave way, Peter jumped and escaped injury, but mother and daddy were caught under the car. Daddy was dead when they found him, but mother lived almost a day."

I had grown callous to suffering and trouble as I approached middle age, but my heart was touched as it never had been before. I slowly patted the white hand in an effort to disclose my feelings, but I'm afraid the child has never known the depth of them to this day.

"You see," she continued bravely, "it was because daddy died first that mother's will and not his became valid, and in it she left everything, including the home at Pine Grove where Uncle Albert lives, to me. Daddy bought it in just recently, because Uncle Albert had mortgaged it so heavily that it was to be sold and daddy wanted to keep it in the family.

"Uncle Albert was furious when he heard mother had made you my guardian. He begged and begged me to marry him. I was raging, and threatened to write you all about it. Then he lured me to the country. He wrote that he was very ill, and I believed him. Watkins told me everything immediately. He said Uncle Albert had sent you a fake telegram, and he had seen him put something in the whiskey, but he, Watkins, had filled it with water, so it would not hurt you. I was frantic—every exit in the wing of the house where I was imprisoned was locked. Dear, dear, I was frantic —about midnight I seemed to feel mother's presence beside me impelling me to go to your assistance. I heard something that sounded like a pebble hit the glass in my window. At first I was afraid to look out. It was Watkins, and he threw me a rope. I quickly tied one end to the radiator, and made my escape. As I flew through the corridor I felt a hand clutch me. It was Uncle Albert. He told me he would kill me if I let you know we were in the house. Then—in this terrible second of desperation you found me."

"The brute," I muttered between my teeth. "He wired me to come and help search for you—that you had eloped with a man who wanted your fortune, but that he had a clue and wanted me to help solve it."

"Don't you see," she replied, "he had carefully planned to poison you, and then he was going to force me to marry him, for without father he had absolutely no means of support."

"And he was taking the line of least resistance," I thought—"the line that leads to nowhere."

"Heavens, what do you think he was going to do with me, Don Compie?"

I never recall having seen such a look of appeal and terror registered upon the face of any other person in my life.

"My little Ellen," said I, holding the two hands firmly in my own, "do you know I loved your mother very dearly? I always wanted the right to protect her, but it was denied me—your daddy won out. She is gone, but you are left. Will you trust yourself to my care?"

She answered with a look that meant more than words—a look that I would have given my soul to have had from another twenty years before.

We washed the dishes, closed the old man's door and started toward our destination, for I had resolved to find Ellen comfortable quarters with a companion before I finished the affair with Albert.

The rain had ceased and there was a peculiarly clear, cool freshness in the atmosphere for a day in August. The hills that surrounded the farm house made clear scallops of green against a pure blue background, and it was hard to believe that turmoil and trouble could exist in such quiet, pleasant surroundings.

We were commenting upon the peacefulness of the scene when an ambulance approached over the hill before us. The road was unusually rough and narrow, a typical country road edged with chinquapin bushes and dogwood trees, whose leaves had already started to turn scarlet, hiding clusters of berries beneath them.

The ambulance swayed from side to side and heeded not the ruts or stones in its wake. As "coming events cast their shadows before," I was quite confident of its destination. I motioned to the driver who gave me a sharp glance and held the horses in a walk just long enough to inform me quickly of their errand.

"To Mr. Albert Wilbur's," was the answer to my question.

"Dead?" I asked.

"Don't know, a servant 'phoned that he had tried to commit suicide."

"Take us back, we're related," I said.

We returned to the house from which we had fled—to find that the two shots, which the misguided man had fired, had done their work only too well. There remained but the frame of him who had given nothing and taken all.

As for myself, I was left alone in the world with this gentle, naïve child, and I prayed each day that she would be more generous with her love than her mother had been—and she was.

It was like a gift from heaven sent to heal a wounded and longing heart.

THE REPORTER.

I made the journey in a motor painted grey—a stylish one upholstered in velvet, and there were things inside to blow and touch for convenience. Be not disillusioned—it did not belong to me. It and the chauffeur were loaned for the occasion by my married sister. Yes, of course, married, because I believe that was what she married for. Anyway, I sat back in this rapidly moving equipage, looking, I believe, very comfortable, but feeling, I am sure, very—now just how did I feel, not very, but "ante turban trepidat." I was shaky and overcome with the same feeling that one has when about to make his first public speech, or at least as I imagine one would feel. However, we had reached the outskirts of the city; the air was pungent with ozone and there was a wafting fragrance of woods—just woods.

I carried the directions of my destination in my hand, written on a slip of white paper. "Keep straight ahead on Falls Road, turn west from Lake Avenue to first road running north; then turn east. First house to the right," the paper read. We had ridden but a short distance after leaving the city—entirely too short for me to compose myself, when the first house to the right began distinctly to outline itself on the horizon. The feeling of trepidation which possessed me intensified itself as we drove up to the door and stopped. Two dogs appeared and barked, but did not approach me. I say they did not approach me, yet the only thing I was entirely certain of that second was a black crepe that hung from the door; it appeared blacker than black, because a bunch of snow white roses unrelieved by green leaves caught the folds and held them.

My fingers shook in an endeavor to separate one of my visiting cards from the pasty tissues that divided them, but they stuck closer than a mustard plaster. Before I was ready the door was opened by a neatly dressed, middle-aged colored woman. Without glancing at me or my card she informed me that Professor Symonds could not be seen.

But I insisted I must, I really must see him. She then scrutinized me closely, she looked me through and through, and I saw she was completely fooled. I was suffocated with shame when I thought of my subterfuge, for I had attired myself in deep mourning—an outfit left from a recent period of mourning after my brother's death, as was also my black-edged card.

"But, honey, he's 'tirely done give out. I knows he won't see no-body."

"I've come so far, do inquire," I pleaded.

"Well, jess you wait here and I'll see. He's right in there," she said, pointing to a room nearby with her head.

"Mayn't I just go in, he'll not mind," I lied.

"You sure, Miss?" the look in her eyes adding force to the question.

"Quite sure."

I followed her as she turned the knob on the sacred door and announced me. She opened it a bit wider. I was close behind, and before anything else happened I was in.

Professor Symonds looked handsome; that was because he was sitting down. His nose was large, but well shaped. Perhaps, after reflecting somewhat, I should say it was a bit too long. His forehead was just an ordinary forehead. But his eyes—let me see, they were of an indescribable color, and his lashes were very long—either long or his eyes were deeply set. I think it was both that gave me the impression. You see I was only sent to interview him and I tried not to stare. Besides it was his mouth that I wanted to look at, and in fact I am conscious now of having looked too hard, but his mouth was decidedly crooked. When he laughed it was more so, but his teeth were large, white and straight. So on the whole it did not detract from his appearance, but I had a keen inclination to hold his mouth and force him to smile straight. Smile I say, but I had only seen him smile once and then very slightly. What I really wanted to do was to coerce him, but it could not be done; he was thinking—thinking of something that was not conducive to smiles.

He arose slowly to greet me. Arose, as one disturbed most unwillingly. While rising he screwed the top on his fountain pen and leisurely adjusted it to his inside pocket. He received me kindly but with manifest annoyance. His face reddened when I told him my mission, and he walked deliberately away from me after I became seated. This discouraged me, but I noticed to my complete satisfaction that he was not handsome—he was not handsome and his clothes were not a good fit. I was glad of these facts, because when I entered the room there was something in the atmosphere, something intangible about the melancholy figure that excited my sympathy and even made my heart beat quicker. But now I saw plainly from his demeanor—his utter indifference—that he regarded me only as a reporter. This was why I was glad to see he was just a short, homely man.

I said, "I hope you'll pardon my intrusion at this trying hour. I was compelled to come for an interview."

"Interview! How extraordinary, when a man's wife is lying dead." His air of surprise did not deceive me, for I knew that many reporters had preceded me. But I felt hurt in my whole being at the rebuff. How could I justify myself for having to confront him at this hour—for this indelicate visit. My color rose, I rose, and the temperature rose. For a moment I could not speak; when my voice returned I replied humbly, most humbly, "The editor gave me the assignment, and I try never to fall down on my job. You must know that it is hard—quite as hard for me as it is for you." I felt all at once the fact that in my effort to succeed in my business I had overlapped conventionalities too rashly.

"Damn editors, they have no feeling for anyone," he muttered; then asked my pardon. I bowed my head and tried to look more modest than a reporter can look.

I saw now that I had a slight chance of procuring an interview, and strange as it may seem I was beginning to like him again. He was entirely uncommon and the possessor of a face embroidered with lines from study and sorrow, and a composure that was calm but forceful.

Ill at ease as I was I made up my mind to stick and see the thing through. A "scoop" like this for my editor meant more for me than I can explain on paper. I pretended to be moving for the door, but wasn't; it was only another subterfuge—the forced weapon of a reporter. Such things are not meant to beguile; but they are a slight means of delusion. So unless you are adapted to the use of them do not apply for a reporter's job.

Professor Symonds slowly walked back from the window, which was not far, because the house was a cottage and the rooms small.

He looked at me squarely, slightly pityingly, for I am sure he was sorry that one so young could be so bold. As for myself I was thinking that perhaps I should live to be an old, old lady—thin scrawny people generally do; but never should I forget with what pride and exultation I had received this assignment. It was first given to Mr. Tyler, our best reporter and our most vivid writer. He failed completely in his efforts to communicate with Professor Symonds, even after he had resorted to detective work. From him it descended step by step to me. Descended most describes the process, for I was a journalist just starting my career and this was the first important piece of work that I had received. Hence my resolution to remain immutable in my decision to stick for the information that my paper so desired. Previous to this affair the majority of my best literary efforts had suffered an evanescence into the world at large. Perhaps John, the janitor, knew of their whereabouts—he always emptied the waste-baskets.

"So you wish me to talk for publication, do you; to lay the facts of my life open to the criticism of the public?"

"No, I—I—"

"Well, I shall do nothing of the kind. The lives of myself and family are entirely my own affair, and no one need count on my giving the papers material with which to fill up their columns."

"But—but the affair was important."

"Important or not, it is mine and with me it shall die. It's a shame, a shame I say, to send young girls to pry into one's private life." It was evident that this speech was from one who could suppress his feelings no longer. Nevertheless, I had grown hot and indignant at his words. At the same time I was becoming alarmed at the nearness of the door to me. This in a way prevented my pungent remarks from having the effect they otherwise would have had.

"If I were allowed to choose my assignments, Professor Symonds, I assure you I should not have chosen this one." This retort was, perhaps, a trifle impudent, considering the fair treatment I had at first received, but it was made without thought, and I was sorry as soon as I realized what I had said.

His speech had caused him remorse, for he was no longer cold and phlegmatic. His attitude of aloofness changed suddenly and completely to fatherly kindness, which made itself felt as he tendered his apologies and again offered me a chair. It was my turn to assume indifference, for I saw now that I was mistress of the situation. I drew myself in, so to speak, smiled a hurt smile and seated myself.

"I thought you might throw a bit of light on Mr. Milton's death," I ventured again.

"The man is dead, why not let it go at that," he suggested, for by this time he had become docile and his attitude suggested capitulation.

"But don't you see," I explained, "it's my assignment, and I must take back something. If it doesn't go with me you'll only be harassed by others. Why not say just what you know?"

"Do you expect newspaper work to get you anywhere?" This was partly to change the subject, and partly to manifest some interest in me.

"Indeed, yes," I replied, "the practice lays a foundation for better writing. Of course, there are things about it that I hate, such as this, but on the whole it is good for one. You see there is no waiting for an impulse to write, which seldom comes naturally to one. The work is there and it must be done. This forced writing teaches concentration and rapidity, while at the same time it keeps one awake to the movements of the day, nationally and internationally." This was from my heart, for it was for this reason alone that I had associated myself with the press.

"Perhaps," he said, "perhaps, but it robs girls of their modesty, and it teaches them to exaggerate events." This brutally frank statement brought me perilously to the verge of tears. At the same time it brought the realization that this particular piece of news—if I succeeded in my purpose—must be reported correctly in every detail—there could be no exaggeration. And I wondered why I cared.

These thoughts must have shown in my eyes. There must have been something about my expression that made my friend sorry for me. I say friend, because I felt from this moment that he was my friend.

"But, of course," he went on, "there are always exceptions. I know you are one and I hope you will remain one." I thanked him and renewed my efforts to worm the desired information out of him. He explained that his aversion to newspapers was due to the pain he had but recently suffered from a great sorrow.

"Had I been a rich man instead of a poor professor there would have been no scandal published about my wife."

"How could you have prevented it?" I asked innocently. I was not innocent, for I had heard much of papers being bought off by advertisers.

"By buying them off."

"Then the story was true, was it not?"

His face reddened, he realized his admission.

"You are the first reporter who has been permitted to enter this house. I have treated you with courtesy and I trust you will spare me any further humiliation in this affair." Such an appeal—it came straight from his heart, but how could I befriend him? I felt myself becoming entangled in a desperate situation. All that he said was true, but on the other hand I had been requested to handle the case carefully and procure the interview at any cost.

I had no doubt that I could obtain the story now, Professor Symonds was my victim or my friend, whichever I wished to make of him. The event rested with me; yet I could not forget with what confidence and assurance I had received the assignment together with full directions for finding the house. Where would I end? I played carelessly with the beads around my neck, pulled my hat a little further to the side, pretended to catch my veil tighter, and then smoothed the wrinkles out of the arms of my gloves; but I could not decide which road to take.

Professor Symonds was longing for a friend—a sympathizer. He was dying to talk—to unburden himself, and the moment seemed propitious. He gave an appealing look and without further protest began to talk.

"This is the story. I give it to you. Do with it what you will." From that second, with me, love took the place of admiration, and I knew that he knew the story was safe.

"It is true that my wife eloped with Milton." As he uttered these words his emotion overpowered him, and he dropped his head in his hands. It affected me so painfully that I tried to restrain him from harrowing his feelings any further. But it seemed as if he understood the sympathetic attitude of his visitor, and wished to confide in me. He continued:

"But there were circumstances that caused it. She was a good woman, a really good woman, but our tastes were entirely different. She loved the city and its closeness to 'things'; I loved the country and its freedom from noise. She loved people; I loved solitude. And besides these differences there were things which you are too young to understand."

I had the natural curiosity of woman and her native diplomacy. So I did not interrupt the continuity of his thoughts.

"Both men and women have strongly developed or even instinctive sex complexes and the physical call of a mate transcends the restrictions that herd instinct places upon our modern society. In other words, it is the elemental appeal that is too strong for the system of barriers society has thrown around modern life. We were congenial, yes, loving and loved, but our natures differed; our habits had not grown together, so our ways parted through no fault of either. Our emotional structures also differed, and the instinctive emotions dominated. Perhaps you will think this explanation incongruous, but I know it to be the truth, and the result of it all is what I am now facing. I see now that my selfishness was chiefly responsible. I was, by nature, the stronger of the two; it was in my power to influence my wife, but we drifted and the realization of the situation came too late.

"In her loneliness she had appealed to Milton and he responded. In him she found a companion with a kindred spirit. They both loved life and what it brought. Now that they are both dead there is only one thing I can do for them, and that is to preserve their reputations, and save them from the disgrace of a disclosure. The public only knows, from the letter found on Milton, that they loved each other; it does not and shall not know more." His head was bent and his voice filled with anguish.

"If I had only known sooner I believe I could have saved her the tragic end. She was returning to me—returning to me, I am confident, for she had entered the garden before she swallowed the poison."

I still did not speak or move and he talked on without a pause. But now he seemed to pull himself together, and I could see an increasing air of satisfaction and gratification in his demeanor, as he found himself confiding in a hearer who was growing more and more sympathetic.

"It is evident that Milton had left her. It was what such propensities always lead to and only what I had expected. Life to be successful must be regular and conventional. We humans are too susceptible to the opinions of others to ignore for long any irregularities, and, as I say, he had left her and gone to Washington. Perhaps he was returning to his wife or perhaps he had just grown tired; anyhow he had reached there before he heard that Helen was dead. He probably thought I'd kill him, so he saved me the trouble.

"Dear, dear, how I should love to do something for you," I said involuntarily, urged by the flood of sympathy the tragic tale had evoked. Then I realized that Professor Symonds might misunderstand me and think my remark too forward.

"It isn't a situation to be envied, is it?"

43

When he asked the question I was thinking of life and its perplexities; the happiness and sorrows that circumstances render without the power on our part either to aid or alter. Here was a man of rare intellectual qualities, a pleasing personality, position and—best of all—a soul; yet he, like others, must live and suffer apparently through no fault of his—but through the thoughtlessness of a pleasure-seeking wife. My sympathy was spontaneous. Is it any wonder that a warm friendship sprang up between us?

And is it needless to say there was no "scoop" for the paper? In fact, my days with the press were numbered. The little cottage needed a feminine touch, and I needed all the love Professor Symonds could give me. Yet I have never been able to fathom why he married me, for my eyes were dark but not luminous; my hair was light, not golden; I was thin and bony; I was tall, yet not erect; I wanted to be wise, but had lots to learn.